This Book is Given with Love

To: _____

From: _____

ISBN: 978-1-957922-29-4
Edition: July 2022

For all inquiries, please contact us at:
info@puppysmiles.org

To see more of our books, visit us at:
www.PuppyDogsAndIceCream.com

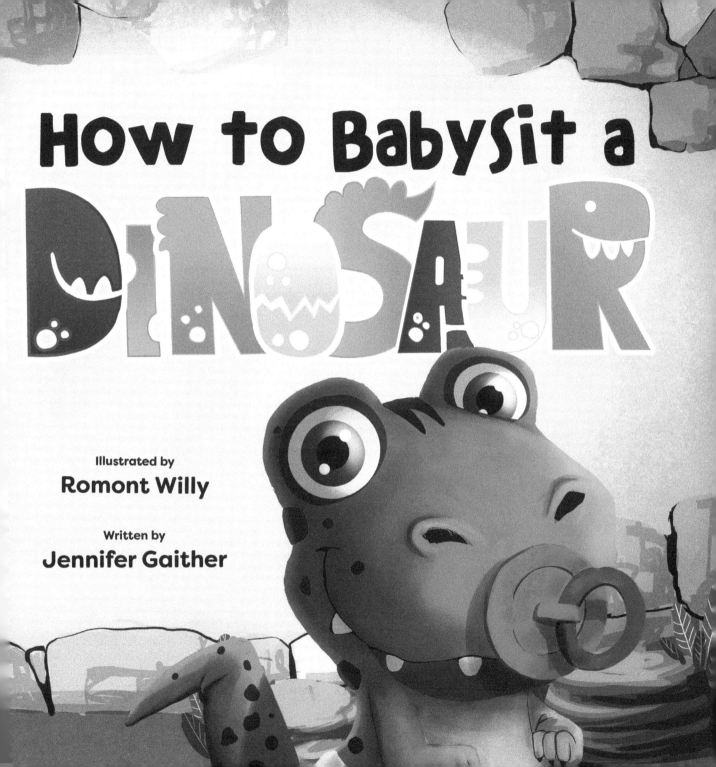

How to Babysit a DINOSAUR

Illustrated by
Romont Willy

Written by
Jennifer Gaither

The office phone rings, a new call is coming through,
"You've reached The Babysitters... How can we help you?"
Mr. Rex **BELLOWS** out, "Can you help us with our tyke?
We're in need of a sitter, while I golf with the wife."

"Mr. Rex, you're in luck," the reception lady replies,
"For your Baby Rex, I'll send one of our best guys.
Steve likes spending time exploring the outdoors,
And he's great with REPTILES, he'll take care of yours!"

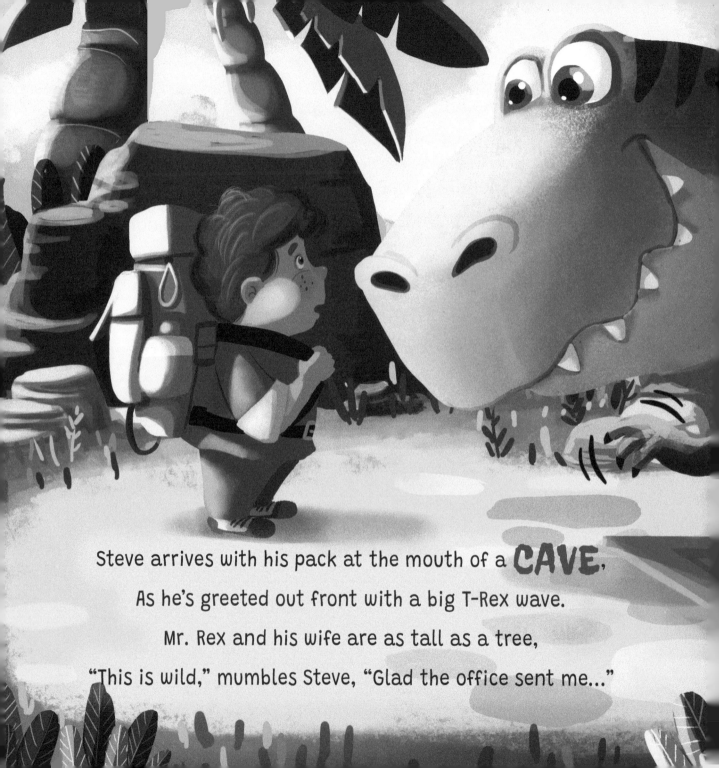

Steve arrives with his pack at the mouth of a **CAVE,**

As he's greeted out front with a big T-Rex wave.

Mr. Rex and his wife are as tall as a tree,

"This is wild," mumbles Steve, "Glad the office sent me..."

"The rules in our household: We listen to mother,
We don't roar at neighbors, and NEVER eat others."
They kiss Baby Rex, "See you later tonight!"
Steve looks at the baby and swallows his **FRIGHT**.

"Let's play!" Steve calls out, leading Rex to the yard,

But gentle play with a dino proves to be hard.

A T-Rex can't catch, 'cause balls **POP** in his claws,

And he's too big to wrestle,

plus, there are those jaws...

Forget hide and seek, his tail gives him away...

Stacking blocks is a challenge... What can a Rex play?

Steve tries to play **chase**, but baby wants to attack.

Guess it's time for a break, so Steve makes a snack!

A predator's diet is mainly all meat,

And you wouldn't believe how much babies can eat!

The pounds this kid **guzzles** are sure to impress,

The kitchen's destroyed so Steve cleans up the mess.

The baby is covered with food head to toes,
So into the bathtub that messy Rex goes!
A quick towel rub will stop the wet-dino stink,
Then a brush for Rex's teeth, and he spits in the sink.

Putting on PJ's is no easy feat,

But Steve's a commander who will not retreat!

SMALL arms and BIG noggin, how will it all fit?

Although baby wiggles, Steve simply won't quit!

As baby refuses, he grows more upset.

This job is the hardest that Steve has had, yet.

The force of his tantrum **SHAKES** rocks from the cave,

"Calm down Baby Rex, please try to behave!"

"You have some big feelings, and I understand,
It's hard to stop playing, but here, take my hand.
Let's take some deep breaths, we can calm down together.
I promise your parents won't be gone forever."

Rex wipes away his tears, and Steve reads him a book,

Then, at last, baby yawns and gets that sleepy-eyed look.

With a head that grows heavy, and pillows piled HIGH,

Baby drifts off to sleep to Steve's sweet lullaby,

The parents come home, and they're happy to know
That their baby is snoozing, "Steve, how did it go?"
"Your baby's a TREASURE, we got along well.
He's sure got a temper, but at least he won't smell!"

No job is too large for our brave Babysitters,
When a family's in need, you know they won't be quitters.
They listen and play, and adapt to each child,
They can handle it all, no matter how **WILD**.

Claim your FREE Gift!

 Visit:

PDICBOOKS.com/Gift

Thank you for purchasing

How to Babysit a

and welcome to the Puppy Dogs & Ice Cream family.
We're certain you're going to love the little gift
we've prepared for you at the website above.

CPSIA information can be obtained
at www.ICGtesting.com
Printed in the USA
BVHW021933130822
644533BV00018B/186

9 781957 922294